SMITHSONIAN INSTITUTION

Smithsonian Prehistoric Zone

# Sabre-tooth Tiger

*by Gerry Bailey*
*Illustrated by Trevor Reaveley*

## Crabtree Publishing Company

www.crabtreebooks.com

# Crabtree Publishing Company

## www.crabtreebooks.com

**Author**
Gerry Bailey

**Illustrator**
Adrian Chesterman

**Editorial coordinator**
Kathy Middleton

**Editor**
Lynn Peppas

**Proofreader**
Kathy Middleton

**Prepress technician**
Samara Parent

**Print and production coordinator**
Katherine Berti

**Library of Congress Cataloging-in-Publication Data**

Bailey, Gerry.
  Sabre-tooth tiger / by Gerry Bailey ; illustrated by Trevor Reaveley.
    p. cm. -- (Smithsonian prehistoric zone)
  Includes index.
  ISBN 978-0-7787-1814-7 (pbk. : alk. paper) -- ISBN 978-0-7787-1801-7 (reinforced library binding : alk. paper) -- ISBN 978-1-4271-9705-4 (electronic (pdf))
  1. Saber-toothed tigers--Juvenile literature. I. Reaveley, Trevor, ill. II. Title.

QE882.C15B35 2011
569'.74--dc22
                        2010044497

**Library and Archives Canada Cataloguing in Publication**

Bailey, Gerry
    Sabre-tooth tiger / by Gerry Bailey ; illustrated by
Trevor Reaveley.

(Smithsonian prehistoric zone)
Includes index.
At head of title: Smithsonian Institution.
Issued also in electronic format.
ISBN 978-0-7787-1801-7 (bound).--ISBN 978-0-7787-1814-7 (pbk.)

    1. Saber-toothed tigers--Juvenile literature.
I. Reaveley, Trevor  II. Smithsonian Institution  III. Title.
IV. Series: Bailey, Gerry.  Smithsonian prehistoric zone.

QE882.C15B33 2011        j569'.74        C2010-906962-5

## Crabtree Publishing Company

www.crabtreebooks.com        1-800-387-7650
Copyright © **2011 CRABTREE PUBLISHING COMPANY.**
All rights reserved. No part of this publication may be reproduced, stored in a retrieval system or be transmitted in any form or by any means, electronic, mechanical, photocopying, recording, or otherwise, without the prior written permission of Crabtree Publishing Company. In Canada: we acknowledge the financial support of the Government of Canada through the Canada Book Fund for our publishing activities.

**Published in the United States**
Crabtree Publishing
PMB 59051
350 Fifth Avenue, 59th Floor
New York, New York 10118

**Published in Canada**
Crabtree Publishing
616 Welland Ave.
St. Catharines, Ontario
L2M 5V6

Printed in China/012011/GW20101014

# Dinosaurs

Living things had been around for billions of years before dinosaurs **evolved**. Animal life on Earth started with single-cell **organisms** that lived in the seas. About 380 million years ago, some forms of animals came out of the sea and began to live on the land. These were the ancestors that would become the mighty dinosaurs.

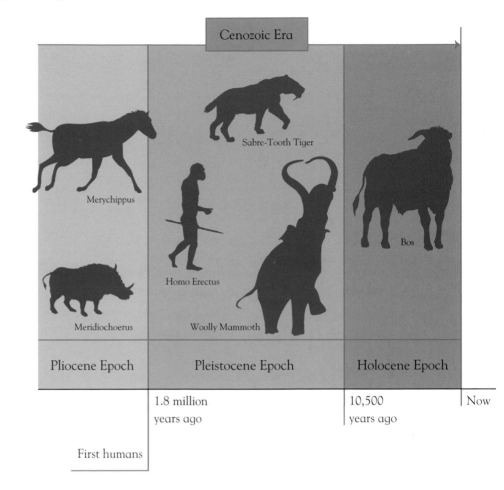

Cenozoic Era

Merychippus

Sabre-Tooth Tiger

Homo Erectus

Meridiochoerus

Woolly Mammoth

Bos

| Pliocene Epoch | Pleistocene Epoch | Holocene Epoch |

1.8 million years ago

10,500 years ago

Now

First humans

The dinosaur era is called the Mesozoic era. Prehistoric animals lived during the Cenozoic era that came afterward. It is divided into epochs, which are periods of time marked by special characteristics. The Pleistocene epoch lasted from 1.8 million years ago until 10,500 years ago.

Sabre-tooth tigers lived during the late Pleistocene period, when herds of bison roamed huge grasslands. Early humans lived during this time too. There were no dinosaurs. They had all become extinct. Mighty **mastodons** lived in the colder climates. They were often **prey** for these wild cats. Sabre-tooth tigers became extinct around 10,000 years ago.

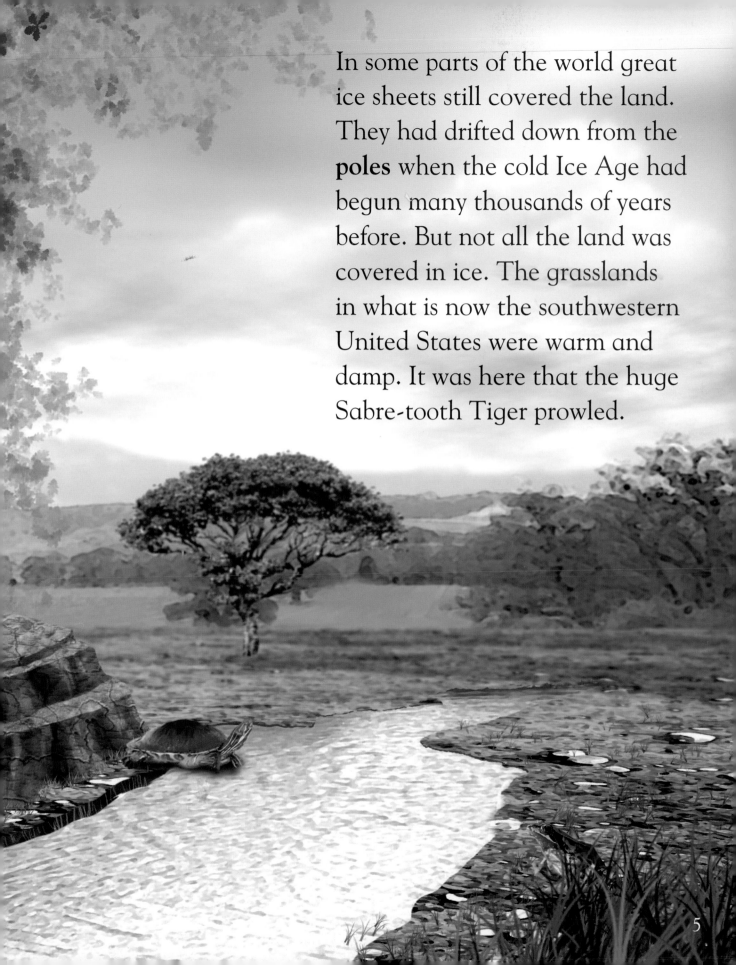

In some parts of the world great ice sheets still covered the land. They had drifted down from the **poles** when the cold Ice Age had begun many thousands of years before. But not all the land was covered in ice. The grasslands in what is now the southwestern United States were warm and damp. It was here that the huge Sabre-tooth Tiger prowled.

He was a magnificent cat. He had strong muscles and powerful jaws. His hearing was very keen and he could pick up a noise coming from far away.

Sabre-tooth Tiger caught the sound of dire wolves. Dire means threatening, and these wolves were ferocious. They were much larger and more powerful than the gray wolves of today. These fierce animals roamed in packs. They were Sabre-tooth Tiger's enemy. He had been forced to fight them in the past when they had tried to steal his food and **territory**.

Sabre-tooth Tiger let out a loud warning roar.
His two long sabre-shaped teeth glinted in the sun.
They were oval rather than round. They had **notched**
edges at the back to give them more strength.

This allowed him to pierce flesh more easily.
But he had to be careful. If he bit down on
something hard, such as a piece of bone, his
sabre teeth could snap.

The sound of the wolves had called the rest of Sabre-tooth Tiger's group. They would hunt as a team now. A pack of sabre-tooth tigers could bring down large prey. A single animal could not.

They moved off in the direction of the howling wolves. Their short, powerful legs could help them **pounce** on an animal, even if they were not especially fast runners.

The wolves were on the other side of a lake. But
this was no ordinary lake. Under the surface water
lay a bed of sticky tar. A mastodon, its huge tusks
held out of the water, struggled to free itself.

It had become stuck. Sabre-tooth Tiger
watched as the mastodon sunk slowly into
the tar. The wolves watched too. So did
the hungry vultures flying above.

The fierce dire wolves watched the helpless mastodon. Then one wolf sprang into the water after it. As the wolf approached, it too became bogged down in the sticky tar.

Now the vultures watched as the two animals
fought for their lives. Both would become **victims**
of the tar pits. Soon these **scavenger** birds would
be able to feed off the flesh of the dead animals.

Sabre-tooth Tiger watched as well.
He was becoming hungrier. The trapped
animals would make a very tasty meal
for him and the members of his pack.

Carefully he dropped one paw into the lake.
But it did not feel right. As his paw began to
sink into the sticky stuff below the water he
sensed danger and backed away.

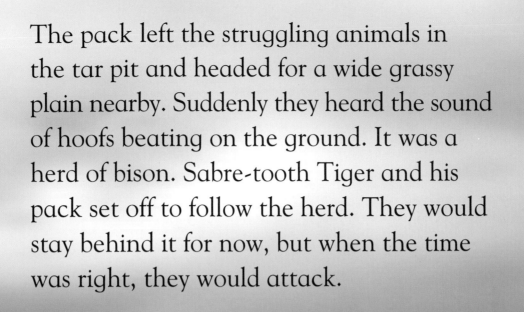

The pack left the struggling animals in the tar pit and headed for a wide grassy plain nearby. Suddenly they heard the sound of hoofs beating on the ground. It was a herd of bison. Sabre-tooth Tiger and his pack set off to follow the herd. They would stay behind it for now, but when the time was right, they would attack.

The bison were large animals with sharp
horns that could pose a danger even to big
cats. Sabre-tooth Tiger never attacked a
strong, healthy animal.

In most bison herds, there was a slower member of the herd or a sick one that would **lag** behind the rest. Sabre-tooth Tiger would single out this animal, **stalk** it, then use his strong legs to pounce on it.

As Sabre-tooth Tiger slowed down to watch the
grazing bison, his sharp eyes picked out another
animal in the woods nearby. It was a huge plant-
eater with long claws called a Harlan's ground sloth.

The ground sloth was busy munching on plants.
Sabre-tooth Tiger was hungry enough to take
on the big ground sloth by himself and risk
being scratched by those claws.

The surprised ground sloth did not stand a chance.
When the pack saw what Sabre-tooth Tiger was
doing, they left the herd of bison and rushed to join
him. The ground sloth provided enough food and

energy to satisfy everyone in the pack.
Now, with his stomach bulging, it was time
for a rest. Sabre-tooth Tiger lay down out of
the sun and yawned. Soon he was fast asleep.

# All about the sabre-tooth tiger

The sabre-tooth tiger was a cat-like animal called a *Smilodon*, which means "knife tooth." It lived during the late Pleistocene period, which lasted from 100,000 years ago to 10,000 years ago. Humans lived on Earth at the same time as *Smilodon*.

The sabre-tooth tiger's **canine** teeth were long and sharp. They also had notches at their back edges to make it easier to pierce flesh. They were oval-shaped to give them extra strength. Unlike modern cats, the sabre-tooth's jaws opened very wide, more than 120 degrees. This allowed the tiger to jab its teeth more easily into the body of its prey.

| Precambrian Era | | 570 million years ago | | | Palaeozoic Era | | |
|---|---|---|---|---|---|---|---|
| Precambrian Period | | Cambrian Period | Ordovician Period | Silurian Period | Devonian Period | | Carboniferou |
| | | | | | 380 First life on land | | 320 First reptiles |

The sabre-tooth tiger was powerfully built, with short legs and a short tail. Really fast animals normally have a long tail to help balance them when they are running. So, scientists believe the sabre-tooth tiger was built for pouncing on its prey rather than running it down at top speed.

It probably hunted slow-moving animals with thick skin, such as bison, **mammoths**, and mastodons. It may have used its teeth to wound its prey in the side. Then, if a bite to the neck did not kill it quickly, it would wait for it to bleed to death.

**Fossils** of sabre-tooth tigers have been found in Europe, North America, and South America. Scientists have studied fossils found in tar pits and **specimens** found frozen in ice sheets. They also study cave drawings of sabre-tooth tigers made by the early humans who may have hunted them.

| | 248 | | Mesozoic Era | | 65 | Cenozoic Era | Now |
|---|---|---|---|---|---|---|---|
| Period | Permian Period | Triassic Period | Jurassic Period | Cretaceous Period | | | |

1.8
First humans

# Tar pits

Around 25,000 years ago crude oil **seeped** up to the surface in an area on the west coast of the United States where the city of Los Angeles stands today. Over time, the oil had **evaporated** leaving pits of sticky tar.

Often a layer of water formed over the tar. Animals who came to the lake to drink did not know what was under the water. The thirsty animals sank into the dangerous tar and became stuck.

Animals stuck in the goo looked like easy prey for predators, such as wolves and sabre-tooth tigers. But the predators would become stuck too when they entered the pit. They were not as smart as later **carnivores**, such as lions.

More than 2,000 sabre-tooth tiger skeletons have been found in the Rancho La Brea tar pits in California and almost the same number of dire wolf fossils. These predators would have entered the pit to catch animals, such as mastodons, that had become trapped, only to become trapped themselves. Scientists have used the fossils of the big cats and dire wolves, as well as other animals trapped in the pits, to study what they looked like. They can build up a picture of what life must have been like at the time.

# Knife tooth

All members of the cat family have two long, sharp teeth located at the front of their upper jaw. These are called canine teeth. They use these to kill prey and tear off flesh to eat.

The sabre-tooth tiger **developed** extra-long canine teeth that dropped down from its top jaw to below its bottom jaw. Its mouth opened very wide, at an angle of over 120 degrees, so the large teeth could be driven firmly into its victim's body.

The sabre-tooth tiger had strong muscles in its shoulders and back. It could lunge downwards with its powerful head and drive its teeth forward.

There were dirk-tooth cats too. They had knife-like canines. scimitar-tooth cats, such as *Homotherium*, had shorter, flatter canines that curved backward like a **scimitar** blade.

# Glossary

**canine** A sharp, pointed tooth on either side of the front teeth

**carnivore** An animal that eats meat

**develop** To grow

**evaporate** To change from a liquid into a gas or vapor

**evolve** To grow and change through time

**fossil** The hardened remains of an organism that lived thousands of years ago

**lag** To fail to keep up

**mammoth** A prehistoric animal from the elephant family, often covered with hair; now extinct

**mastodon** A prehistoric animal similar to an elephant, which is extinct today

**notch** A v-shaped cut

**poles** The north or south end of Earth's axis

**pounce** To jump down on something suddenly

**prey** An animal that is hunted by another animal

**scavenger** An animal that feeds on the bodies of dead animals

**scimitar** A sabre with a blade that curves outward

**seep** To slowly spread or trickle through

**specimen** A sample used for study

**stalk** To track, or follow, prey

**territory** An area of land

**victim** A living thing that suffers or is killed

# Index

bison  19, 20, 22, 24, 27
canines  26, 30, 31
Cenozoic Era  3
claws  22, 23
dirk-tooth cat  31
fossils  27, 29
Harlan's ground sloth  22, 23, 24
*Homotherium*  31
ice sheet  5, 27
knife tooth  26, 30
legs  10, 26
mastodon  3, 12, 13, 14, 27, 29
Mesozoic era  3
Pleistocene period  3, 26, 27
predator  28, 29
prey  3, 10, 26, 30
Rancho La Brea  29
scavenger  15
scimitar-tooth cat  31
*Smilodon*  26
tar  12, 13, 14, 28
tar pit  15, 19, 27, 28, 29
teeth  8, 9, 26, 27, 30, 31
vultures  13, 15
wolves (dire)  7, 10, 12, 13, 14, 28, 29

# Further Reading and Websites

*Saber-Toothed Cats* by Susan Heinrichs Gray. Child's World (2005)

*Saber-Toothed Cat* by Marc Zabludoff. Benchmark Books (2010)

**Websites:**

www.smithsonianeducation.org